名流詩叢 7

黃昏時刻

The Hour of Twilight

李魁賢◎著

黃昏的時刻已到
樹林把一片入暮的蒼茫
投落在塔的遠方……

自　序

　　自從與國際詩壇有所接觸，提供詩創作的外譯，尤其是英譯本，做為交流的媒介，成為必要的前題。起初是由策劃人邀請擅長外文的詩人朋友代勞，後來有朋友垂青拙作，比較有系統翻譯，迄今出版過日文、英文、葡萄牙文、羅馬尼亞文、俄文、希臘文、蒙古文等詩集，產生實質的詩交流效果。

　　2007年前往印度青奈出席世界詩人大會，我起意想自己整理一冊英譯詩集做為比較完整資料，提供給各國的詩人朋友，我一鼓作氣翻譯了70首，正好權充自己虛度70歲月的砥礪，這就是《黃昏時刻》的由來。

　　《黃昏時刻》裡有一部分詩，朋友譯過，我自己重譯或修改。譯者通常會受到原作的拘束，而作者自己則比較方便揮灑，這是我從俄羅斯詩人布羅茨基（Joseph Brodsky, 1940-1996）自譯詩獲得的經驗，微妙的細節也是作者比較容易拿捏。另外一部分則是第一次有英譯本出現，或是自己的偏愛，或是新作，尚無機會獲得方家外譯。

《黃昏時刻》還未在國內出版之前，設在蒙古的世界詩歌年鑑出版社已搶先選擇其中40首，在2009年初以蒙英雙語版印行。茲為方便國內讀者的指教，承秀威同意以漢英雙語出版，真是一舉兩得。檢視這些詩篇寫作時間竟然橫跨四十年（1966-2006）之久，雖不免有白雲蒼狗之感，惟寫作時的感受心情依然歷歷在目，躍躍在心。

本書首句恰好出現「黃昏的時刻已到」，順手得來成為書名，豈非天意？黃昏時刻多少有些落寞，而進入暮境更是滄然蕭瑟，然而晝夜循環，一日之計在於晨，若未雨綢繆，何嘗不可視為翌日之計在於暮呢？英文Twilight恰好又有晨、昏、微明、薄暗，雙重意義。而詩之妙悟，正是求之於微言大義。

四十年前一首詩的詩句，成為四十年後一本書的書名，顯示詩緣在寰宇之中，無處不在。個人進入二十一世紀後，在國際詩壇上，尤其與印度和蒙古的密切交往，更深深感受到詩的交流，就是心的交流，是無遠勿屆的緣份，而詩緣正是令人感到最幸福的所在。

2009.07.15

塔

黃昏的時刻已到

樹林把一片入暮的蒼茫

投落在塔的遠方

用妳軟軟的手去探測水的根源

那消息是在水鏡的背面

好似一閉鎖的錦匣

難以預測的季節的幽徑

就好似那蒼茫封住的塔

永恆的生命在此靜立

就好似　啊　終究在深邃的根源

樹木舉起　指向入暮的天空

殘暉呼嘯而去

蒼茫落在妳的眼前

妳的影子啊　必定要長大

妳探測的軟軟的手啊

必定也要塑造一座孤立的塔

1966.05.18

Tower

The hour of twilight is coming

The woods cast a vast obscurity of dusk

faraway behind the tower

Your soft hands search for the water source

which is disclosed behind the water mirror

like secluded path of an unpredictable season

Like the tower surrounded by obscurity

an eternal life stands quietly here

as if, ah, eventually from a deep source

the trees lift up toward the evening sky

When the faded sunlight roars away

dusk falls before your feet

Oh, your shadow must grow up

your soft searching hands

must also erect a lonely tower

1966

教堂墓園

是誰引導我來到此地
和你對晤　享受你周遭的寧靜

早春的陽光　聖樂的歌聲
是川流不息的噴泉　灑落在
你企圖捕捉的手掌上

父母不朽的愛心　又點燃兩支
紅紅的燭光
天使幼嫩的翅膀在你的碑石上
閃現出 RETO 1961-1962 的字樣
玫瑰　黃菊以及紫羅蘭的遊伴
環繞在你的身旁

啊　你的生命已然永存

在歌聲與笑語的年紀

我可以用你初學的語言同你把晤

啊　我也已然死過

卻不能和你同在

永死的國度

1967.03.05

Churchyard
——*Kathedrale, Chur*

Who leads me over here

to meet you enjoying the surrounding serenity

Sunshine of early spring and sound of sacred music

are endless fountains sprinkling onto

your catching palms

Eternal love of your parents again

lights two candles

The angels with tender wings on your tombstone

display the words " RETO 1961-1962 "

Roses, yellow chrysanthemums and violets

are your companions around you

Ah, your life exists forever

at the age of song and laughter

I can talk with you in your mother tongue

Ah, me too died once

yet unable to join you

in the state of eternal death

1967

不會唱歌的鳥

起先只是好奇

看鋼鐵矗立了基礎

接著大廈完成了

白天　窗口張著森冷的狼牙

夜裡　窗口舞著邪魔的銳爪

對著我們的巢

因為焦慮　聲帶漸漸僵硬了

有如空心的老樹

於是人類在盛傳：

鳴禽是一種不會唱歌的鳥

1969.06.02

Un-singing Bird

At first, it was just out of curiosity

observing the erection of steel framework

then the accomplishment of whole building

By day at the window, it displays terrible wolf teeth

by night at the window, it dances with devilish sharp claws

toward our nests

Because anxious our vocal cord is gradually stiffened

like a hollow old tree

Hence, people broadcast extensively :

The oscine is a kind of un-singing bird

1969

回憶占據最營養的肝臟部位

回憶是孤立的煙囪

一到黃昏

就吐著濃濃的煤煙

存在於語言之前

這虛無的生活狀態

起先就把不住的風向

往往向東向南向西向北

飛鳥般悠然擴散

回憶是流動的陷阱

把吐出的煤煙

又誘引進來

好像捉迷藏時在門檻跑出跑進的孩童

而自得其樂

這樣　一到秋天

回憶變成了癌

占據最營養的肝臟部位

一面坐吃肚空起來

1969.06.03

Memory Occupies the Best Part

Memory is a lonely smokestack

emitting dark smokes

in the evening

This insubstantial condition of living

exists before any language

Without any definite target

the smokes scatter in all directions

like free birds gone with the wind

Memory is a movable trap

releasing the smokes

and gathering them again

like a child running in and out playing hide-and-seek

Then by fall

memory becomes a cancer

occupying the best part in liver

and eating up till all empty

1969

生命在曠野中呼叫

把匕首用力投擲過去
一次又一次
從外圍逐漸向內心集中

他睨視著凶暴的夏天
這樣揮手練習的姿態
竟也逐漸感到暈眩了

生命在曠野中呼叫著
每當他的手垂落
生命在曠野中呼叫著

他凝聚自己形成一把匕首

蓄勢向中心炎熱的牆

做最後的衝刺

1969.06.18

Life is Calling in the Wilds

He throws the knife by force

over and over

gradually converging to the center

He stares at the violent summer

in such a practicing action

finally becoming dizzy

Life is calling in the wilds

whenever his hand suspends down

life is calling in the wilds

He concentrates himself as a knife

making the last dart with full power

toward the hot center on the wall

1969

鸚 鵡

「主人對我好！」
主人只教我這一句話

「主人對我好！」
我從早到晚學會了這一句話

遇到客人來的時候
我就大聲說：
「主人對我好！」

主人高興了
給我好吃好喝

客人也很高興
稱讚我乖巧

主人有時也會
得意地對我說：
「有什麼話你儘管說。」

我還是重複著：
「主人對我好！」

1972.02.16

Parrot

" *My master is kind to me!* "
My master teaches me this word only

" *My master is kind to me!* "
I practice this word by day and night

Any visitor comes
I shout
" *My master is kind to me!* "

My master is so pleased
to give me nice foods and drinks

inviting many visitors in appreciation of

me being smart and clever

Occasionally, my master

quite elatedly says to me

"Speak whatever you think!"

I still consistently repeat

" My master is kind to me!"

1972

野　草

大地呀　擁抱妳的時候

感到全身痙攣的溫熱

有我的血　有我的汗

在底層躍動的生命

使我滿山遍野地歌唱

迎著陽光　歡呼明日的序幕

在荒野擁抱妳的身體

難道是宿命的存在嗎

我們常被阻絕在大路的兩旁

因為路上有轔轔的車輪輾過

有喧嘩的山羊成群拉出不消化的屎粒

有哭喪的嗩吶對著虛空吹響

親切體驗在野地裡自由自在的擁抱

彼此依偎著溫熱的愛心

大地呀　我知道

妳不會計較在我的擁抱下隱藏身份

我們的宿命是唱出嘹亮的歌聲

歌聲才是我們存在的價值

愛才是我們存在的真諦

1977.09.19

Weeds

O earth, when we embrace you

we feel warmth running through our bodies

along with our blood and our sweat

The life active underground

makes us sing over mountains and plains

We welcome the sunshine and hurrah for tomorrow

Is it our destiny

to embrace you in the wilderness

We are often separated by the road

where the wheels rumble on

the noisy goats drop their undigested excrements

and the flutes in funeral cry against the vacant sky

In the wilderness we freely embrace each other

closely together to gain warm affection

O earth , we realize

you will not feel ashamed when we embrace you

it is our destiny to sing loud and clear

Singing is the only sign of our existence

Love is the only real meaning of our existence

1977

兩　岸

愛的暗潮不自覺地
充滿我們不能跨越的距離

我們兩岸從同一個山嶺的起源
不自覺地各自奔赴前程
無形的水面蒙蔽我們河床一體的命運
距離常是變幻的風雲
即使有一天拉遠到看不見的異域
那種壯闊的汪洋仍展現愛的真實

距離相近會有激起波濤的顧慮
有攪動渾濁的怨嗟

但不論河面如何洶湧

愛是以底淵的深度衡量

我們的距離有不能跨越的神聖

不管是南岸風光　北岸蕭瑟

美的風景是和諧不是一致

愛的情意是深沉不是浮動

1977.09.23

Two Banks of a River

The secret tide of love unconsciously

fills up our gap that no one can pass over

We both originate from the same mountain

but each unconsciously rushes to respective goal

The unity of our fate is obscured by the water surface

There is always a variable distance between us

yet in case of probably diverged out of sight

we can still find love in the vast ocean at last

There is a worry about being too close

probably to cause the water turbid

But no matter how turbulent it is on the surface

the love is measured by the depth of riverbed

The distance between us that no one can pass over is sacred

in spite of south bank flourish and north desolate

The beautiful scenery is harmonious rather than uniform

and the true meaning of love is calm rather than hasty

1977

弦　音

來吧　來打擊我

我是熱火熬煉的陶甕

裝滿溫暖的血液

來吧　重重打擊我

讓我的血液從破裂的傷口

流下甦醒的天空

澆潤滿山的杜鵑

來吧　來打擊我

我是烘爐熔鑄的鐘鼎

禁錮澎湃的聲響

來吧　重重打擊我

讓我的聲響從震撼的胸膛

傳播晨起的山崗

呼應滿天的雲彩

來吧　來打擊我

我是不死不滅的大地

瀰漫自由的風雨

來吧　重重打擊我

讓我的風雨從開闊的原野

滋潤新綠的心靈

彈奏滿懷的弦音

1981.12.22

Sounds of Strings

Come on, come to hit me

I am a pottery pot smelted by hot fire

and filled with warm blood

Come on, come to hit me hard

let my blood flows out of cracked wound

down streaming over the morning sky

pouring on the wild azalea all over the mountain

Come on, come to hit me

I am a bell forged by a blast furnace

and restrained in depth with roaring thunder

Come on, come to hit me hard

let my sound springs out of my vibrating breast

broadcasting over the awakening hills

to find echo in the colorful clouds

Come on, come to hit me

I am the earth imperishable forever

and disseminated with wind and rain of freedom

Come on, come to hit me hard

let the wind and rain sweep across spacious plane

moistening the souls of new green

to touch the strings finding an echo in heart

1981

舞　龍

蜿蜒曲折的身姿
彷彿流傳的歷史一樣

我們以身體語言
描寫綿綿無盡的起伏
印證祖先溫熱的心

火炬的光明
永遠在前面引導

1982.10.20

Dragon Dance

The body in undulating movement

resembles a circulated history

With our body language

we describe the prolonged rising and falling

verifying the passionate minds of our ancestors

A torchlight perpetually

leads the team on parade

1982

那霸之冬

用曾經持槍和握佩刀的手

已經不見了的手

以不銹鋼代替的畸形的手

支撐在被傷害過的大地

跪在那霸街頭

墨鏡可以防止太陽光的暈眩

草綠軍帽使光頭

永遠免對羞於相見的天

手風琴哀怨著

終戰前地下決死戰壕內

被軍國主義所剖腹自裁的同志

哭泣的心

用殘軀向誰控訴呢

軍機一批一批呼嘯劃空而過

青少年一批一批喧嘩橫街而過

1983.01.05

Winter in Naha
― *Okinawa 1983*

With the hands once gripping the gun

holding the sword

with the hands already missing

yet replaced by abnormal artificial limbs

of stainless steel

propped up on the once hurt earth

the retired soldier of survivor

kneels on the street of Naha

wearing sunglasses to prevent himself

from being dizzied by sunshine

and a grass green helmet to shield his bald head

always bent away from the heaven

which he is ashamed to face

He plays his accordion

with a grieving and mournful tone

for his combatant comrades who committed suicide

at the end of World War II

under provocation of militarism

and died in the battle trenches underground without exit

To whom might his weeping heart appeal

with only this one remaining torso

Yet the fighters still zoom on the sky

squad after squad

while the teenagers still clamor across the street

flock after flock

1983

雪　天

我感覺那地層的胎動

當圍攏過來的烏雲愈積愈厚

開始有了雪花

嫩枝被寒冷壓彎了腰

忍不住就把重擔的雪

彈回風中飄散

在愈冷的時候

才會感覺大理石的肌膚

有溫泉一樣的地熱

我要開花給無人看

落花生一般結果

在始終暖和的地層下

1983.01.27

Snowy Day

I feel the quickening of the strata

when dark clouds crowd around incessantly

and snowflakes begin to fall

Tender branches weighed down with cold

cannot help bouncing back the snow into the air

scattering it in all directions

Only when it is getting colder

can one feel the skin of marble

as warm as a spring of earth thermal

I would like to bloom for no one

and bear fruits like groundnuts

under the ever warm strata

1983

愛還是不愛

當他突然閉口不語的時候

我不知道愛還是不愛

纏綿之後

應有一些倦態吧

風聲

一陣又一陣

在淡淡的月光下

看到自己略微鬆弛的肌膚

是否愛也會隨著鬆弛呢

彷彿聽到遠去的腳步聲

回頭看到他的臉

嚴肅得令我感到

愛的莊嚴

不管愛還是不愛

我心底的微笑

浮上來

1983.02.11

Loves me or not

When he suddenly keeps silent

I do not know whether he loves me or not

After making love

should it be a little tired

The wind sounds

once and again

Under pale moonlight

I find my muscle slightly loose

and wonder his love will be loose too

The steps seem going far away

I turn to look at his face

a solemn expression making me

the feel of love a solemnity

No matter he loves me or not

a certain smile emerges from

the depth of my heart

1983

訊　息

魚在砧上解剖時

剩下鱗片

在閃光

好像向遠方打信號

傳遞

愛的訊息

1983.04.27

Message

When fish being dissected on the chopping board

the remaining scales

are glistering

as though signaling for distance

to transmit

a message of love

1983

我一定要告訴妳

我一定要告訴妳

啤酒從妳的嘴裡

溜到我嘴裡的感覺

真美妙

摻雜著冰冷和溫暖

即使有　些

會不慎溜到床單上

妳把斜向天空的紙糊拉門

闔上　把陽光

關在外面

因為免受監視

感到安全

把時代周刊放在一旁

我們看金瓶梅的影片吧

不要　還是讀詩吧

這樣有些頹廢的浪漫

我們抓住了輕飄飄的自由

但那監視的電子眼還在

不是裝在屋子裡

好像是在身體內的某部份

和風濕症一樣

啤酒從妳的嘴裡

溜到我嘴裡的感覺

是序曲

也是間奏

試想把自由放大　除非

打開天窗

忽然　報社的爆炸聲

我聽到心裡有人受傷的

呻吟聲　我感到

整個天空都在監視

我的愛

我一定要告訴妳

真的

摻雜著溫暖和冰冷

1983.04.28

I Must Tell You

I must tell you

It is beautiful

the feeling of icy wine flowing

from your mouth into mine

It mixes up cool and warm

though some drops are inadvertently

fallen on bedclothes

You shut the sliding grated paper door

inclined opening to the sky

keeping the sunshine outside

and feel secure owing to

preventing ourselves from watching

Put aside your Time magazine

Let us play the movie of erotic romance

No, let us rather read poetry

enjoying something romantic and decadent

We grasp the drifting freedom

before the hidden electronic eyes

which are mounted nowhere in the room

but become part of our bodies

just like suffering from rheumatism

The feeling of icy wine flowing

from your mouth into mine

is an overture

as well as an intermezzo

We cannot imagine how to extend our freedom

unless we open the skylight

Suddenly, from the explosion of newspaper head office

I hear in my heart

the moans of somebody injured

I sense

the entire sky is watching us

My love, I must tell you

it really admixes

cool and warm

1983

輸　血

鮮血從我體內抽出
輸入別人的血管裡
成為融洽的血液

我的血開始在別人身上流動
在不知名的別人身上
在不知名的地方

和鮮花一樣
開在隱祕的山坡上
在我心中綻放不可言喻的美

在不知名的地方

也有大規模的輸血

從集體傷亡者的身上

輸血給沒有生機的土地

沒有太陽照耀的地方

徒然染紅了殘缺的地圖

從亞洲　中東　非洲到中南美

一滴迸濺的血跡

就是一頁隨風飄零的花瓣

1983.08.11

Transfusion

Blood is drawn from my body

and transfused into vessel of any other

becoming a new harmonious stream

My blood begins to circulate within other body

within the body of unknown person

at somewhere unknown place

Just like the fresh flowers

blooming on the secluded hillside

an unspeakable beauty blossoms in my heart

At somewhere unknown place

there is also transfusion on a large scale

from the bodies of collective massacred

Transfusing blood into the waste land

a place of no sunshine

is in vain to dye the fragmentary map red

From Asia, Middle East, Africa to Latin America

a drop of splashing blood

represents a petal gone with the wind

1983

巴黎之冬

香色麗舍燦爛的夜空

是遊客流連的巴黎

小妞也不忘兜售異鄉人的慈善

「Monsieur　給您一朵紅玫瑰！」

我老漢的巴黎

卻是傷兵醫院牆角外

這一片雜亂

野貓跳過垃圾錫桶時

滾蛋似的乒乓聲

是我的麗都秀

蒙瑪特脂粉味的海風

是流浪水手忘返的巴黎

小鬼也勤於推銷異鄉人的慈善

「Monsieur　給您一朵紅罌粟！」

我老漢的巴黎

卻是自從阿爾及利亞轉進後

剩下的這把亂髭

唔　這裡還有一個啤酒罐

可恨抬頭就會看到那艾菲爾鐵塔

高高高高的塔尖刺破我飄浮在那上面天空中的氣
　　球心

1984.06.21

Winter in Paris

In Paris, what the tourists hanker for

is a magnificent night sky over Champs Elysées

A lass never forgets to peddle charity for foreigners

" Monsieur, a red rose for you ! "

From old fellow eyes of mine, the Paris

is but this disorderly place outside of

the wall around the Hôtel des Invalides

When a stray cat jumping across garbage tin drum

its rolling rattles are

my Lido show

In Paris, what the wandering sailors are fascinated with

is the sea breeze mingling with cosmetic perfume at

    Montmartre

A lad is also diligent to push sales charity for

    foreigners

" Monsieur, a red poppy for you! "

From old fellow eyes of mine, the Paris

is but this unkempt beard remained after

withdrawing with troops from Algeria

Well, here is another beer can

What I hate is looking up to see the Eiffel Tower there

with a high, high, high peak bursting my balloon

    heart aloft in the sky

1984

秋末的露台

大麗花

痴痴地開了一個下午

在秋末的露台上

披一身陽光

像刺蝟

脫掉了裝飾的綠葉

什麼都不是

就是乾乾脆脆的花

漸漸地

我也會脫掉花瓣

脫掉陽光

甘願為他開

一生

在無人的

露台上

1984.10.16

A Balcony in Late Autumn

A dahlia with sheer infatuation
has bloomed throughout the afternoon
on the balcony in late autumn
wearing the sunlight all over the body
like the spines of a hedgehog

Throwing off the decorative green leaves
it is nothing else
but a crisp and straightforward flower

Gradually
I will throw off all my petals
throw off all sunlight

I am willing to bloom for him

all my life

on the balcony

none around

1984

留 鳥

我的朋友還在監獄裡

不學候鳥

追求自由的季節

尋找適應的新生地

寧願

反哺軟弱的鄉土

我的朋友還在監獄裡

斂翅成為失語症的留鳥

放棄語言　也

放棄海拔的記憶　也

放棄隨風飄舉的訓練

寧願

反芻鄉土的軟弱

我的朋友還在監獄裡

Resident Birds

My friends are still in the prison

They do not emulate the migratory birds
pursuing the season of freedom
in search of an adaptable new place
and would rather
feedback to their feeble homeland

My friends are still in the prison

They rest wings to become resident birds of aphasia
giving up their language
their memory of above sea level

their practice of adrift flying

and would rather

ruminate on the feebleness of their homeland

My friends are still in the prison

1984

檳榔樹

跟長頸鹿一樣

想探索雲層裡的自由星球

拚命長高

堅持一直的信念

無手無袖

單足獨立我的本土

風來也不會舞蹈搖擺

愛就像我的身長

無人可以比擬

我固定不動的立場

要使他知道

我隨時在等待

我是厭倦遊牧生活的長頸鹿

立在天地之間

成為綠色的世紀化石

以累積的時間紋身

雕刻我一生

不朽的追求歷程和記錄

1984.12.16

Betel Palm

Like a giraffe

I grow higher and higher

trying to explore the planets behind the cloud

I persist a straight consistence

with neither hands nor sleeves

standing up independently with only one foot

no dancing and no wavering compliant with the wind

Love is so long as my height

no one comparable

My standing point is so immovable

to let him understand that

I am all the time waiting for

As the giraffe tired of nomadic life

I stand on earth under heaven

transforming myself into a green fossil of century

tattooed on my body with accumulated time marks

to engrave the immortal process and record

of my pursuit in all life

1984

楓　葉

楓葉

是自由的勳章

帶著泣血的骨肉

頒給雪封不死的大地

大地剩下枯枝的手

還要努力戳破紙糊拉門一樣

沉甸甸謊言自由的天空

天空還是一樣的天空

但在世紀的嚴寒中

還有陽光紅潤的地方

還有流水的琴弦

伴奏鳥語花香

還有堅持秋色的楓葉

楓葉

是愛的勳章

帶著他的體溫

在我自己封存的雪地上

1985.01.19

Maple Leaf

A maple leaf

is a medal of freedom

with bone and flesh of weeping blood

bestowed to the undying earth covered by snow

On the earth only withered branching hunds are left

still striving to pierce the false freedom of sky

no more than sliding grated paper door

Sky is still the same old sky

yet in the severe coldness of the century

there is somewhere with reddish sunshine

the stream sounding like music of string

singing of birds and fragrance of flowers

the maple leaves insisting an autumn scene

A maple leaf

is a medal of love

with the warmth of his body

casting to my snowy land sealed by myself

1985

圍　巾

圍巾是手的延長

纏繞在我的項際

脖子像伸出海面的潛水鏡

在寒風中破空前進

他的手纏繞在我的項際

把體溫留給我身體

雲是圍巾的延長

飄動在山岳的項際

山在凝眸對視的流浪中

凝固成為日記上剪貼的紙花

他的圍巾飄動在我項際

把風姿留給我窗前

愛是雲的延長

醞釀在情人的項際

晚霞是時間壓縮的煙火

在空間呈現無限膨脹的浪漫

他的懷念醞釀在我項際

把名字留給我喃喃自語

1985.01.30

The Scarf

The scarf wrapping around my neck

is an extension of his hand

My neck like a periscope on the sea

moves forward breaking the cold wind

His hand wrapping around my neck

gives me his warmth

The cloud drifting around the mountain neck

is an extension of the scarf

Wandering mountain stopped under the loving stares

becomes a paper flower pasted on my diary

His scarf drifting around my neck

leaves a graceful poise in front of my window

The love brewing around the lover neck

is an extension of the cloud

The sunset cloud being a temporally compressed

    firework

displays in the space with boundless romantics

Remembrance of him brewing around my neck

entwines his name murmuring in my heart

1985

幽　蘭

　　像受傷的蝴蝶一般

　　離梗落在

　　手術台上的蘭花

　　被百葉窗間隙落入的陽光

　　覆上囚衣的條紋

　　有如流行的瘟疫

　　蘭花紛紛落下

　　成為焦土中的部落

　　在等待著魂回故鄉前

　　一絲不自由的溫暖

我的愛也像

受傷的蝴蝶一般

享有一絲不自由的溫暖

在百葉窗帘的下面

1985.05.03

Secluded Orchid

Like a wounded butterfly

fallen from the stem

a flower of orchid lies on the operation table

covered with the stripes of a prison uniform

as sunshine casted through the blades of venetian

>   *blind*

Like a kind of spreading epidemic

the flowers of orchid fall pell-mell

resembling the tribes on the scorched sites

waiting for a breath of restricted warmth

before the souls return to their homelands

My love too

just like a wounded butterfly

enjoys a breath of restricted warmth

under the shade of venetian blind

1985

費城獨立鐘

銅鐘裂了

在費城

看自由鐘聲

遠在荒蕪歷史中

斑駁

我卻一直想著

你的自由

何時會從遠方

傳來

期待

你的愛會敲出鐘聲

寫出自由的歷史

在地球上的

任何角落

1985.07.16

Independence Bell in Philadelphia

The bronze bell has cracked

In Philadelphia

the bell of freedom

is mottled in the forsaken

history

I am thinking about

when your freedom

will resound

from afar

I expect

your love will toll the bell

sounding history of freedom

to find an echo

in every corner of the world

1985

詩人之死

詩

發表的時候

只有

一張紙的

重量

加上

一些油墨

加上

一些多氯聯苯

黑黑的

跟你的皮膚

一樣

掉落時

差不多像樹葉

無聲無息

詩人莫魯士

你

被吊在

絞首台上

處死的時候

用生命

寫成

最後一首詩

在人間的

天平上

比整個地球

還重

一頭是

你靜靜垂下來

枯萎的花

另一頭

是搖晃動盪起來的

地球

詩人莫魯士

你

被吊在

絞首台上

處死的時候

像東方節慶的

一盞月亮

不

實際上

一盞花燈

火燒燈

熊熊蔓延起來

照耀

黑色大陸的

黑暗

地球另一半的

黑暗

1985.10.23

註：　莫魯士（Benjamin Moloise）是南非詩人，因反對南非白人政府的
　　　種族隔離政策，1985年被處絞刑。

The Death of a Poet

Poetry

when published

is merely weighed

no more than

a piece of paper

incorporated with

some inks

further with

some polychlorobiphenyl

in black color

just as

your skin

and soundless

almost like the leaves

as fallen

Poet Benjamin Moloise

you

when hanged on

the hanger

to death sentence

are writing

with your life

one last poem

weighed greater

than whole globe

on the balance

where one side

being your silently suspending

faded flower

and opposite side

the vibrating oscillatory

globe

Poet Benjamin Moloise

you

when hanged on

the hanger

to death sentence

are just like

a moon

in oriental festival

no

in effect

a flower lantern

burnt

brilliantly wide-extended

to illuminate

the darkness

in black continent

the darkness

in another half globe

1985

Note: Benjamin Moloise was a poet of South Africa and hanged to death in 1985 by Afrikaner government due to his opposition to apartheid.

痲瘋

「我全身痲瘋！」

你這一句話

沒有一絲怨嗟

只感到

你溫熱帶的陽光

使萬物努力成長

蒼翠立在

歷史的海洋中

你沒有因屈辱

早生白髮

颱風頻傳

地震不息

你獨臂

也能撐過多少苦難

你的清白

依然如赤子之心

大家竟然

連你的名字也

不敢提

真的把你

當痲瘋病人一樣

因為你的名字

是：台灣！

1987.03.28

Leprosy

" *My all body suffers from leprosy！* "

you say this word

without a little bit of complaint

rather give us an impression

that you have subtropical sunshine

keeping all living things energetic

Verdantly standing on

the ocean of history

you do not grow premature gray hairs

as subjecting to insult

The typhoon comes frequently

the earthquake vibrates intermittently

you even have only one arm

capable to endure so many troubles

Your innocence

is still like the mind of a maid

yet no one actually

dares to mention

just your name

rather treats you really

like a leprosy victim

simply because your name

Taiwan !

1987

黑森林的陽光

傳說

我的黑森林裡

有世紀的漆暗

莽莽蒼蒼

一片不知所終的

歷史幽徑

傳說不知

我有明朗的

等高線

坦蕩蕩的

山和谷

和流水

最豐收的是

陽光

和寧靜

中傷的萬箭

穿胸

長成耐寒心的

杉

在天空

寫流雲

寫愛的詩句

過濾污染

傳佈的

風言風語

我起伏的

山巒裡

沒有虎豹豺狼

只——有

溫馴的小鹿

偶爾

急急躍過

林中結網的公路

像一道　也是

陽光

1987.09.09

The Sunshine in the Black Forest

It rumors

that in my black forest

there is darkness of centuries

full of immense chaos

and a secluded path of history

leading to nowhere

The rumor is ignorant

that I have clear and distinct

contour line

with mountains and valleys

and flowing streams

The most bumper harvest is

sunshine

and serenity

Thousands of hurting arrows

pierce my chest

and grow up as cold-resistant

pines

to depict drifting clouds

and the words of love

in the sky

filtering the pollution

and spread of

chattering winds

Amid of my wavy

mountain range

no tiger, leopard or wolf

but

the meek deer

occasionally

jump swiftly across

netted highways in the forest

just like a ray of

sunshine

1987

晨　景

鳥聲

叫醒雲

雲

叫醒太陽

太陽

叫醒旗

旗

叫醒了天空

1988.01.24

Morning Scene

Birds

wake up the cloud

Cloud

wakes up the sun

Sun

wakes up the flag

Then, flag

wakes up the sky

1988

愛情政治學

我企求

愛情

可獨立於婚姻的統治之外

妳堅守

愛情

要獨立於性行為的統治之外

我們只是認知

不表示同意或不同意對方的立場

首先

是我逾矩

違反外交的禁忌

妳的抗議

使我體會到

我所信仰的愛情似有似無

愛情也許只是虛幻的籠罩

我反省而恍然領悟

精神生活的立場

應該獨立於愛情的統治之外

才能獲得充分靈性的自由

我釋放自己

感到壓力鬆弛後的平靜

失去了張力和彈性

像一條沒有彈力的橡皮筋

呈現虛脫的狀態

望著喪失感覺的歷史真空

沒有翻案的欲求

還不如蚯蚓

可以隨意翻翻佔有的領土

我終於明白

內在自由的誕生

要甘願獻身於愛情的束縛下

成為不後悔的囚徒

禁閉自己

期待鐵門終有打開的一天

終能獨立於龐大陰影的統治之外

1988.06.11

Politics of Love

I expect

love

may be independent of the reign of marriage

You insist

love

is independent of the reign of sexuality

We simply acknowledge rather than express

to agree or disagree the standpoints of opposite party

First of all

it is me going beyond the principle of compromise

violating the taboo of diplomacy

Your protest

makes me realize that

my faith in love seems to be or not to be

Perhaps the love is nothing but an illusory expression

I introspect myself and suddenly comprehend

that the standing of spiritual life

ought to be independent of the reign of love

to obtain the freedom of supreme divinity

I free myself

feeling the calmness after the burden being released

just like an inelastic rubber band

presenting a condition of marasmus

for lack of any tension and elasticity

In face of the vacuum of insensible history

I have no desire to overturn a verdict

even incomparable to an earthworm

capable of turning over its occupied soil at will

Eventually, I understand that

the birth of inner freedom must be

willing to devote oneself under obligation to love

becoming its prisoner of no regret

to confine himself

awaiting someday the opening of iron door at last

to get independent of the reign of tremendous

     shadows

1988

鐘乳石洞
——桂林蘆笛岩

張口

在傳統巨岩鎮壓下

叫喊了幾千年

不惜嘔出肺

　　吐出腑

呈現空無的心機

任你們

隨意進出檢視

終究

只有人類史上熬出的精華

鐘乳石柱的硬骨

依然

梗在喉中

支撐著上下顎

嘶喊著：

還給我的人權

1989.02.23
北京

Stalactite Cave
— at Ludyi Rock, Guilin, China

The wide-open mouth

under the suppression of a traditional huge rock

has been screaming for several thousands of year

not sparing to exhale the lung

        to vomit out of the stomach

for empting the power of my mind

let you as please

enter therein for examination and exit arbitrarily

After all

there is only the essence found in the human history

the stiff bone of stalactitic column

remains firmly

obstructed in the throat

keeping the upper and lower jaws open

 shouting

" *Give me back my human right* ！ "

1989

螭　首
——北京紫禁城

無聲無息

面對擁來擠去的遊客

逐漸風化的裝飾

以虛假的螭首

統一配置

在龐大禁城的牆坦

沒有搖曳的身姿

沒有呼風喚雨的遊戲

在強制規劃的格局下

數百年間

溫馴到和中國人民一樣

張著乾燥的大口

沒有水跡

1989.05.04

Dragon Heads
—— *Forbidden City, Beijing, China*

Voicelessly and breathlessly

facing toward the waves of tourists

the virtual dragon heads

as ornaments of gradual weathering

are arranged uniformly

along the walls of grand Forbidden City

Neither an appearance of swinging gesture

nor a magic show of summoning wind and rain

they are under a forcefully planned disposition

for hundreds of year

so tame as Chinese people

opening their wide thirsty mouths

without a trace of water

1989

杜鵑花

長年禁錮的青葉

一到花季

就展示滿樹泣血的火熱

往年點綴都市叢林中的苞蕾

像螢火蟲一樣

提燈夜遊的精靈

如今東山一把

　　西山一把

滿山遍野就連成一片綠色

用鮮艷的彩色吶喊

喊出燦爛的青春

喊出錦繡的遠景

花落

為了一望無際的香土

1990.03.21

Azalea

Keeping green leaves silent all year round

the azalea bursts into weeping blood fever

at the beginning of blooming season

In the past, the buds scattered among the urban

    bushes

just like the fireflies

the spirits carrying the lanterns wandering at night

now in crowd on eastern hill

then in crowd on western hill

jointed together to arrange a scenery of spring all

    over

The azalea shouts with colorful voices

for brilliant youth

for flourishing vision

The flowers fall

for the purpose to incense the boundless native

   country

1990

黑　雨

黑雨落在沙漠

沙漠變成火山口

黑雨落在海灘

海灘變成營火場

黑雨落在戰車上掛曬的軍服

軍服變成海盜旗

黑雨黑雨直直落

落在心田

心田變成泥濘的沼澤

1991.01.31

Black Rain

Black rain is falling on the desert

the desert becomes a crater

Black rain is falling on the beach

the beach becomes a base for bonfire

Black rain is falling on military uniforms

hung to dry on the tanks

the uniform becomes a pirate flag

Black rain, black rain keeps falling

onto the hearts of people

the hearts become respective muddy swamp

1991

天　禍

拿火箭當做火柴
在天空擦著

這種高危險性的遊戲
連神也離天避難

有人在禱告
可是神離開了
誰都沒聽見

火箭留下
天空受傷的血跡

1991.01.31

Calamity in the Sky

A missile is taken as a piece of match

striking in the sky

This kind of serious and dangerous game

urges even gods escaping from calamity

Some people are praying

but all gods have gone away

so no one heard it

The missile remains behind

the blood stains on the injured sky

1991

無人島

因為是無人島
才成為自由的土地

然而在被稱為自由土地的時候
才是真正淪陷的時刻
鐵靴開始在島上踐踏

島在軍人的統治下
挖戰壕　做偽裝工事
等其他人來搶奪
自由

1991.02.01

A Desert Island

It is a free land

simply because it is a desert island

But at the moment it is declared as a free land

it is going to be occupied

The iron boots begin to trample on the island

The island under rule of the military

is entrenched and carried out camouflage construction

waiting for others coming to sack

the freedom

1991

沙　漠

是誰在沙漠上
架好的槍口
插上春天未到臨前
早開的鮮花

黃沙滾滾
花瓣上有天空的血跡

是誰在沙漠上
啞口的層層荒蕪中
羅列久久猶不肯瞑目的
望著天空的頭顱

黃沙滾滾

眼瞼上有天空的淚痕

1991.02.02

Desert

Who is that in the desert

inserting into the muzzle of a gun

a fresh flower of premature

before the arrival of spring season

Yellow sands sweep all over

Bloodstains from the sky remain on the petals

Who is that in the desert

displaying on the mute desolated land

with dead heads in rows yet opening their eyes

staring at the sky for a long, long time

Yellow sands sweep all over

Tear traces from the sky remain on the eyelids

1991

俘虜與解放

一位戰士被俘虜了

只是一位俘虜

一位女兵被俘虜了

全世界有一半人口成了俘虜

一位戰士倒下了

只是一位解放

一位暴君倒下了

全世界有一半人口獲得解放

1991.02.02

The Captive and Liberation

A warrior is nothing but a captive

after he is captured

but half of the world population would become captives

after a female soldier is captured

A warrior falls

it is nothing but emancipating himself

but half of world population would be liberated

after a tyrant has collapsed

1991

歲　末

看不到燦爛的夜景
裝飾起來的節慶

在反光玻璃圍牆的室內
咖啡的濃香
政治　革命　愛情　性
熱絡的話題
烤著暖和的心

走到街上
歲末的冷風吹著
心漸漸冷下來
腳步漸漸沉重

殘餘的鐵絲網

還留在安全島上

1991.12.19

Year-end

No festival scene is decorated

to display the night brilliant

In the room with stained glass walls

the atmosphere in coffee flavor

Involved in the fanatical topics of

politics, revolution, love affair and sex

warms up our enthusiastic hearts

Walking on the street

the chilly wind blows at year-end

our hearts cool down little by little

our steps are getting heavier one after another

The barbed wires are still remained

on the traffic safety island

1991

給妳寫一首詩

我給妳寫一首詩

沒有玫瑰和夜鶯

在歲末寒流中

只有霹靂的鼓聲頻頻

在歲末寒流中

我給妳寫一首詩

看不到妳的時候

深深感覺到妳的存在

看不到妳的時候

思考我們存在場所的現實

我給妳寫一首詩
信守我們的承諾

信守我們的承諾
期待愛的世紀來臨
在禁錮的鐵窗裡
我給妳寫一首詩

1992.02.04

One Poem for You

I write one poem for you

no rose, no nightingale

but thundering drumbeat urgently

in the cold wave at year-end

In the cold wave at year-end

I write one poem for you

in a deep sense of your present

while you are out at my sight

While you are out of my sight

thinking about the reality of our living place

I write one poem for you

in a faith to keep our promise

In a faith to keep our promise

expecting the era of love to come

behind the iron bars of prison

I write one poem for you

1992

三位一體

擁抱妳的時候

我聞到乳香

好像庭院裡的玉蘭花

在我的清晨

賦有了生命真實的意義

我不容許妳受到輕蔑

因為妳是我的母親

擁抱妳的時候

我聞到鼓聲

好像滿山遍野的杜鵑花

在我的午後

敲擊著生命美麗的旋律

我不容許妳受到侵犯

因為妳是我的情人

擁抱妳的時候

我聞到露水

好像幽谷中初綻的百合花

在我的黃昏

吐露出生命純潔的芬芳

我不容許妳受到委屈

因為妳是我的女兒

1992.02.17

Trinity

Embracing you

I smell the fragrance of breast

as the orchid in the garden

in the morning

giving the true significance of the life

I will protect you from any contempt

because you are my mother

Embracing you

I hear the beating of drum

as the azalea all over the hill

in the afternoon

striking the pleasing melody of the life

I will protect you from any violation

because you are my woman

Embracing you

I feel the freshness of dew

as the lily in the deep valley

in the evening

exhaling the natural flavor of the life

I will protect you from any depression

because you are my daughter

1992

明治村夏目書齋前

陽光來到書齋簷下

生前居無定所的夏目漱石

承繼森鷗外的住宅

終於定居在明治的歷史上

經歷過陰鬱生活的夏目

在櫻花盛開的季節裡

依傍入鹿池的藍天綠水

定居在陽光的故鄉

然而我居無定所的心情

坐在漱石的書齋簷下

感到陽光緩緩跨過我的身上

黃昏帶著涼意跟蹤而至

1992.04.13
白樺湖

In front of Natsume's Study
— *at Meiji Village*

The sunlight comes over here under the eaves of the

    study

Natsume Soseki without definite house in his life

inherited Mori Ogai's once residence

finally has settled in the history of Meiji era

Natsume who had lived a gloomy life

settled at this sunny hometown

accompanied with blue sky and green water of Iruka lake

in the season of cherry blossom

My mind has not found yet a settled place

sitting under the eaves of Soseki's study

I feel sunlight gradually striding across my body

and twilight with a touch of coolness follows

1992

島嶼臺灣

你從白緞的波浪中
以海島呈現

黑髮的密林
飄蕩著縈懷的思念
潔白細柔的沙灘
留有無數貝殼的吻

從空中鳥瞰
被你呈現肌理的美吸引
急切降落到你身上

你是太平洋上的

美人魚

我永恆故鄉的座標

1992.04.20

Taiwan Island

You emerge as an island

from the waves of white satin

The dense forest of black hair

drifts with longing nostalgia

The beach of soft white sands

is imprinted with numerous kisses of shells

Taking a birds-eye view from the sky

the beauty of your texture is so attractive

that I am landing onto your body thirstily

You are a mermaid

in the Pacific Ocean

the landmark of my eternal home country

1992

白髮蘚

只要你堅定不移地

佔有世界上受鍾愛的角隅

我便同樣堅定不移地

依附在你石質堅持的表面

在你火成岩的內層

永遠有暗中輻射的熱情

我青苔地衣廣被你外表的冷峻

靠著你冷中的熱展現我的生機

即使我漸漸轉化成白髮蘚

仍然緊緊和你結合一起

不分晝夜　無論晴雨

即使做為你的裝飾也無妨

1992.07.19

註： 白髮蘚為一種隱花植物，附生於岩石上，為大屯山特殊景觀之
一，因地熱轉白，由青苔逐漸變成白髮狀，故名。

Silver-haired Lichen

As long as you insist immovably

occupying this beloved corner in the world

in the same kind I will insist immovably

attaching on your durable and stony surface

There is always passion secretly radiating

from inner layer of your igneous rock

My green moss covers all over your superficial coolness

to present my vitality depending upon your hot in cold

After having gradually turned into sliver-haired one

I am still engaged with you in close-tightness

day and night, rain and shine

I don't mind even merely as your decoration

1992

Note: Silver-haired lichen grows on rocks and turns gradually from green moss into white color by subterranean heat.

紅杉密林

紅杉的巨木

霸佔了整個天空

陽光照不到厚實的大地

世界寧靜得聽不到

任何風聲雨聲

即使這樣

在封鎖的原始密林裡

即使上千年霸佔一切天空的巨木

也會瞬間轟然倒下

連根拔起

大地上累積厚厚的腐植土

在這些死亡的哀愁底下

赫然有新綠的生命掙扎而出

一個政權倒下

自然有另一個政權崛起

土地並沒有被竊據

它是喪禮的祭壇

也是嬰兒的浴池

雄立的新生紅杉

傲視著倒下的前朝

從表皮開始逐漸解體

以迄魂飛魄散

1992.09.04

Redwood Forest

The giant redwood trees

occupy the whole sky to block the sunshine

from radiating onto the good earth

The world is so quiet

that no sounds of wind and rain can be heard

In spite of this situation

the giant trees of thousand years

occupying whole sky in the blockaded forest

might be fell down and uprooted

at any moment

On the ground accumulated with thick humus soil

there are new greens struggling out

underneath the sadness of dead lives

After one regime has fallen

another regime will rise spontaneously

The land would not be usurped

it is but an altar in funeral

also a bath for new baby

The outstanding fresh redwoods

proudly look down on the fallen dynasty

appearing disintegrated from surface step by step

until disappearing of all soul and sense

1992

傀　儡

他們叫我演什麼

我就演什麼

他們叫我說什麼

我就說什麼

扮演嘴巴的角色

佔住正義講台

我不知道正義是什麼意思

買票的觀眾是什麼樣的心情

我表演過為獨裁者之死而哽咽

為金權腐蝕的政客落選而錯愕

我不知道這是真實的傀儡人生

還是傀儡的真實性格

他們給我妝扮最美好的臉譜

他們給我獨佔偌大的舞台

寵愛的燈光焦點投射在我身上

他們操作我靈活的手腳

讓我耀武揚威　顧盼自雄

他們鼓動給我熱烈的獎賞掌聲

淹沒四方角落此起彼落的詛咒

我不滿自己傀儡的演技嗎

我自承傀儡

還是繼續扮演傀儡

因為我根本就是

傀儡

1993.03.25

Puppet

I play

whatever I am asked to play

I say

whatever I am asked to say

I play the roll of a spokesperson

I occupy the justice podium

but I do not understand what is justice

I do not care about the feeling of audience

I played the role sobbing for the death of a dictator

astonished at their defeat in election of some corrupted

　　　　politicos

I do not know if this is the real puppet life

or the real character of a puppet

I am made up to show a best facial sketch

and given to possess a huge exclusive stage

The favored spotlights focus on my body

My active limbs are manipulated

let me show off and feel my own prowess

I win applause by an inciting big hand

to keep down the curses from all corners

Should I dissatisfy with my own skill

I recognize myself as a puppet

and will go on to play my puppet show

because I am in essential

a puppet

1993

俄羅斯船歌

俄羅斯的民歌

順著涅瓦河的河水流著

船歌　啊　俄羅斯的船歌

迴旋著層層的漣漪

手風琴　曼陀林　搖鼓和響板

組合著俄羅斯　韃靼　高加索

哥薩克　吉普賽和烏克蘭各種民族的交響

音樂的組合也就是民族的組合

蘇聯解體了

六個民族加盟的民俗樂隊

仍然唱著回腸蕩氣的歌謠

仍然和涅瓦河的漣漪一樣

分不出彼此的音域

音樂的融合已經超出了體制

甚至已不只是俄羅斯的船歌

遠到人為藩籬而長期隔絕的台灣人民

也在心裡震盪著層層的漣漪

1993.06.17
聖彼得堡

Russian Boat Songs

Russian folk songs

drift along the water of Dnepr River

Boat songs, oh, Russian boat songs

swirl around the extended ripples

Accordion, mandolin, tambourine and castanets

compose a philharmonic of Russian, Tartar,

Caucasian, Cossack, Gypsy and Ukrainian people

The composing of music composes the races too

The Soviet Union has collapsed

however, the folklore band allied by six races

still sings the folk songs together touching our hearts

just like the ripples on the Dnepr River

undistinguished between one range and another

The combination of music goes beyond establishment

even not only being sung as a Russian boat song

but also rippled extensively in the hearts of Taiwanese

barricaded due to political reason for long

1993

逃 亡

銅像逃亡之後

基座依然

靜立在祕密警察總部前

呈現荒蕪的身段

只有蔓草

代替往日錦簇的花圈

只有枯枝

代替威武的錦衣衛隊

銅像逃亡

基座在

勳章逃亡

歷史在

愛情逃亡

詩歌在

生活逃亡

風雪在

啊啊

逃亡的天空裡

只有雁的悲吟在

1993.12.06

Exile

After the bronze statue has exiled

the base still stands erect

quietly in front of the KGB headquarter

in a desolate pose

The elegant wreaths in the past

are now replaced by wild creepers

The stern imperial guards in smart uniform

are now replaced by withered branches

The bronze statue has exiled

while the base exists

The medal for honor has exiled

while the history exists

The love thing has exiled

while the verse exists

The civic living has exiled

while the snowstorm exists

Oh, oh

in the sky exiled

only the mournful sighs of the wild geese exist

1993

真　相

你可以說不的時候
卻沒有聲音

你可以沒有聲音的時候
卻唱頌歌

你可以唱頌歌的時候
卻吝於吟詠山高水長

你可以吟詠山高水長的時候
卻希望聽到掌聲

你可以聽到掌聲的時候

卻已看不到真相

1993.08.30

Real Facts

When you may say no

you bear no voice

When you may keep voiceless

you would rather to sing praise

When you may sing praise

you are reluctant to appreciate the nature

When you may appreciate the nature

you expect to hear applause

When you may enjoy the applause

you go blind to real facts

1994

不再為你寫詩

我不再為你寫詩了

台灣　我寫得還不夠多嗎

我寫到手指變形

　寫到眼睛模糊

　寫到半夜敲門都會心驚

　寫到朋友一個一個頭髮花白

　寫到所愛的人一個一個離去

台灣　你卻一直渾渾噩噩

　　　水一直流膿

　　　空氣一直打噴嚏

　　　土地一直潰瘍

　　　人物一直政客

我的詩不能做藥方

不能減輕沈疴

本身開始縮水

漸漸枯萎

只剩下不死的心

在等待詩復活

等待那一天

打開天空

看到我們自己的旗幟

聽到我們自己的歌聲

1994.06.10

No More Poems for You

No more poems for you

Taiwan, is it insufficient of my works dedicated to you

    I keep writing until

    my fingers deformed

    my eyesight blurred

    my heart frightened at the midnight door-

        knocking

    my friends having their hairs turned to gray one

        by one

    my loves leaving me far away one after another

Taiwan, you are still indifferent and unconcerned

    water keeps flowing with pus

    air keeps sneezing

land keeps suffering from ulcer

people keep becoming politicos

My poems could not be the prescriptions

unable to relief the chronic disease

even begin to shrink themselves

and dry up day by day

Only my undying heart is left with me

waiting for the resurrection of poetical creations

waiting for someday

opening the sky

our own national flag is seen

our own national anthem is sung

1994

人的組合

本來
朋友是朋友
敵人是敵人
朋友的朋友也是朋友
朋友的敵人也是敵人
敵人的朋友也是敵人
敵人的敵人也是朋友

偶爾
朋友變成敵人
敵人變成朋友
朋友的朋友也變成敵人
朋友的敵人也變成朋友

敵人的朋友也變成朋友

敵人的敵人也變成敵人

結果

朋友不知道是朋友還是敵人

敵人不知道是敵人還是朋友

朋友的朋友也不知道是朋友還是敵人

朋友的敵人也不知道是敵人還是朋友

敵人的朋友也不知道是敵人還是朋友

敵人的敵人也不知道是朋友還是敵人

至於

朋友的朋友的朋友

朋友的敵人的朋友

朋友的朋友的敵人

敵人的朋友的朋友

敵人的朋友的敵人

敵人的敵人的敵人

更分不清楚究竟是朋友

或者是敵人

甚至

朋友的朋友的朋友的朋友呢

……

……

敵人的敵人的敵人的敵人呢

1994.08.30

Combination Among People

Essentially

a friend is a friend

an enemy is an enemy

a friend of a friend is a friend

an enemy of a friend is an enemy

a friend of an enemy is an enemy

an enemy of an enemy is a friend

Occasionally

a friend becomes an enemy

an enemy becomes a friend

a friend of a friend also becomes an enemy

an enemy of a friend also becomes a friend

a friend of an enemy also becomes a friend

an enemy of an enemy also becomes an enemy

Consequently

whether a friend is a friend or an enemy

whether an enemy is an enemy or a friend

whether a friend of a friend is a friend or an enemy

whether an enemy of a friend is an enemy or a friend

whether a friend of a friend is an enemy or a friend

whether an enemy of an enemy is a friend or an

      enemy

Furthermore

a friend of a friend of a friend

a friend of a friend of an enemy

a friend of an enemy of a friend

a friend of an enemy of an enemy

an enemy of a friend of a friend

an enemy of a friend of an enemy

an enemy of an enemy of a friend

an enemy of an enemy of an enemy

it is hardly to distinct

who is a friend and who is an enemy

Eventually

how about a friend of a friend of a friend of a friend

……

......

how about an enemy of an enemy of an enemy of an

enemy

1994

你是蚊子

你儘管抽血吧

儘管咬住你認為甜美的部位

享受你的富足吧

在靜靜的夜裡

用我的血供養你

我不吝嗇

只希望你不要擾亂我的安眠

使我精神恍惚

可是你在飽食之後

還要吵吵嚷嚷

分不出白天還是夜晚

才是令人無法忍受啊

1994.10.08

You are Mosquito

Go ahead and suck my blood

go ahead and bite the best part of my body

enjoying your full satisfaction

in the silent night

Feeding you with my blood

I am not stingy at all

provided do not disturb my sleeping

making my mind blurred and confused

However, what unbearable is

after your eating to the full

you are still making a noise

day and night

1995

與山對話
——挪威利德

山沉默不語
用岩層堅持它的性格

有時候透過鳥的聲音
有時候透過樹的手勢
向村民招呼

只有在雪融的時候
才伸出長舌瀑布
嘩啦啦述說不停
我聽不懂的挪威話

我也沈默不語

學習岩層堅持我的性格

只揮揮手

用眼睛說：「好（gau）早！」

1995.06.19
挪威利德

Dialogue with the Mountain
— *Leadal, Norway*

The mountain keeps silent

in a character of rocky bedding

but says hello to the villagers

sometimes through the singing of birds

sometimes through the gesture of trees

When the snow melts

a long tongue of waterfall stretches out

talking hurrah unceasingly

with the Norwegian language unfamiliar to me

I also keep silent

in my own character learning the rocky bedding

but wave my hands and say with my eyes

" Good Morning " in Taiwanese language

1995

冰河岩
——冰島菲姆沃竺岩

冰河到海口的距離

只是風

冰河時代到海洋時代的距離

只是雪

帶著懷念妳的夢

走過風的世紀

帶著懷念妳的相思

涉過雪的紀元

大西洋啊

我急急奔向妳

數千年才移動寸步

我還是堅定地邁向宿命的至愛

直到妳不再澎湃

我就把整座山的岩層獻給妳

按照原先的約束

不說一句話

1995.06.24
冰島雷克雅維克

Glacial Rock
—— Fimmvörðuhals, Iceland

In the distance from the glacier to the seaside

has nothing but wind

while from the glacial age to the ocean era

has nothing but snow

With the dream of longing for you

I passed through centuries of wind

With the love of longing for you

I waded across the epoch of snow

Oh, you Atlantic Ocean

I am rushing toward you

in a continuous movement by inches for thousand

    years

insisting to reach my best love of destiny

By the time your billows are no longer roaring

I'll dedicate to you all rocky beddings of a mountain

    range

according to our previous promise

without saying any word

1995

馴鹿和白楊
——芬蘭北極圈

白楊學著馴鹿

把樹枝長成鹿角

向天空展示

馴鹿模仿白楊

把鹿角長成樹枝

到處招搖

白楊有時裝成馴鹿

隨意移棲生殖地

馴鹿有時裝成白楊

固定地方休息

馴鹿和白楊在北極圈

彼此變換動靜

觀察稀有人類

偶爾稀有的動靜

1995.07.01
芬蘭伊瓦洛

Reindeer and Poplar
—*Arctic Circle, Finland*

The poplar learns from the reindeer

to grow its branches like deer horns

displaying them to the sky

The reindeer emulates the poplar

to grow its horns like branches

swaggering around everywhere

The poplar sometimes acts like the reindeer

emigrating at will to somewhere for reproduction

while the reindeer sometimes acts like the poplar

resting fixedly in place

The reindeer and the poplar in the Arctic Circle

exchange their habits of activities

looking at the rare action

occasionally happened to the rare human being

1995

矛 盾

人怕人
更怕沒有人

動物因其他動物喪生
更因沒有其他動物而絕種

一種語言喧嘩
多種語言更為吵鬧

騷擾的世界令人難受
沈默的社會更令人無法適應

秋高氣爽好登山

初冬雨中行更能領略人生

1994.11.20

Contradiction

People are afraid of somebody

however, more afraid of nobody

Animals die because of other animals

however, even die out because of no other animals

Monolingual presents an egocentric clamor

however, multilingual performs more noisy

Turbulent would makes anyone uncomfortable

however, silent society is more inadaptable

Good autumn season is suited for climbing the mountain

however, walking in rainy winter is better for

understanding the life

1996

雅典的神殿

多利斯巨柱支撐著

一片神話的天空

神話卻像浮雲一般飄逝

留下巨柱

支撐著歷史的廢墟

沒有趕上歷史的饗宴

現代遊客

紛紛擠進巨柱下的廢墟

把自己裝模作樣的姿勢

拍進歷史的鏡頭裡

每個人都用不同的角度

詮釋神殿的遺址

在唯一不變的世俗天空下

神早已失去了立身的場所

躲進歷史的角落

1993.03.07

Parthenon in Athens

The giant Doric columns

uphold a heaven of myths

The myths drift like floating cloud

leaving the giant columns

to uphold this ruin in history

Absenting from the glorious times in history

the modern tourists but

crowd each other into the ruin under giant columns

taking the picture of their affected poses

into the lens of present history

Everyone explains from different aspects

about the ruin of sanctuary

Under the secular and invariable sky

Gods have lost their own places for existence

and hide themselves at the corners of history

1996

奉　獻
——獻給二二八的神魂

寒流抵才過去

寒流總是會過去

四界有燈火加咱照路

在更較暗的時瞬

咱也知也天總是會光

天光的時瞬

咱會當看著你等流血流汗

奉獻生命　給咱台灣的土地

發到真青翠的大叢樹仔

開到真艷的各種花蕊

過去無疑誤天要光的時

遂變成黑天暗地

過去無想著隔腹的親戚

哪會青面獠牙

你等的苦難就是台灣的苦難

總是　苦難的時代已經過去

你等的生命已經和台灣結成　體

你等的血汗變成甘露水

灌溉台灣豐沛的收成

你等奉獻的生命

創造台灣勇敢輝煌的歷史

因為有你等行過的路

台灣人的子孫

頭殼才會當舉到高高高

因為有你等流過的血

台灣人的子孫

胛脊骨才有法度激到挺挺挺

我唸這首詩奉獻給你等

因為你等已經將你等的生命

奉獻給咱台灣

1999.02.23

Dedication

— *To the victims of massacre in the event on Feb. 28, 1947*

The cold wave has passed over

It should pass over anyway

The lights illuminate our way anywhere

Even at the moment darker than ever before

we believe that the dawn would come soon

When it dawns

we are clear to see your bleeding and sweating

and dedicating your lives to our beloved country

on which the trees grow tall and green

the flowers bloom radiant and colorful

In the past no one doubted that at dawn

it became great darkness between heaven and earth

In the past no one could imagine that our close relatives

would be so brutal and barbarous

Your distress was a misfortune of our nation

However, the time of distress has passed over

and your lives have been combined into our nation

Your bloods and sweats become sweet dews

in favor of the plentiful harvest on our land

Your sacrifice dedicated to the age

creates a history of courage and glory

Because of the path you stepped

Taiwanese descendents

are able to lift their heads

Because of the bloods you shed

Taiwanese descendents

are capable of standing erect

I read my poem dedicated to you

in memory of your lives

having been dedicated to our country ——Taiwan

1999

告別第二個千禧年的黃昏

告別第二個千禧年的黃昏

我看到自己的影像映照在炫目的夕陽裡

過往的努力紛紛擾擾呈現自滿的燦爛格局

迎接第三個千禧年的清晨

對台灣的後代是日照更為絢麗的美景

不是土撥鼠而是松鼠在林中跳躍

坦克　地雷　戰機　火箭　飛彈

人類依賴非理性狀態下夢魘的發明

成為地球上嗜血到兇狠紅眼的異端

回到學習與自然和諧相處尋求人性的再現

有城市的民族　也有農耕的民族

有狩獵野鹿的民族　也有追逐飛魚的民族

山林中本來不是國族主義發祥地

讓梅花鹿回到祖先的地方生息　還有山羌

讓黑面琵鷺高興就來安逸客居　還有伯勞

庭院裡也不是種族隔離的試驗場

美人蕉可以亂彈琵琶　台灣欒樹也可以隨風舞蹈

九重葛可以紅到四季款擺　七里香也可以芬芳到

　　遠近心歡

來不及懺悔的舊時代走過難以自拔的沼澤

迎接第三個千禧年的新時代

讓我們滿懷安心期待你——台灣的後代

1999.09.17

Farewell to the Dusk of the Second Millennium

Farewell to the dusk of the second millennium

I see my own image reflected dazzlingly by sunset

the past efforts confusingly presented to a brilliant

    complacence

Welcome the early morning of the third millennium

a more flourishing vision of sunshine to new generation

It is not the marmot rather the squirrel that jumps

    among the woods

Tanks, mines, fighters, rockets and missiles

the inventions created by human under irrational
    nightmare
become bloodthirsty, ferocious and red-eyed heretics
    on earth

Return to learn in harmony with nature for reappearance
    of humanity
there are urban people as well as agricultural people
there are hunting people as well as fishing people

The forest is not originally the source of nationalism
Let deer return to their ancestor habitat, and also
    wild goats

*Let black-faced spoonbills perch here as guests, and
also shrikes*

*The yard is not an experimental place of racial segregation
Canna plays the balloon-guitar at will and willow
dances before the wind
Bougainvillea grows red all seasons and Rutaceae
transmits fragrance everywhere*

*The old age never for repentance has walked through
the swamp
Welcome the new generation of the third millennium*

let us expect you at full ease — the posterity of New World

1999

黃昏 時刻

山在哭

山在哭　你聽得見嗎

沒有人在傾聽

沒有人知道山的哭聲

現代人不認識山

不知道山會口渴　山會流淚

不知道山會痛　山會癢　山會酸

以為溪澗是山在低語

　　　瀑布是山在高歌

但你聽得見山的哭聲嗎

只會肆意蹧蹋的山鼠

善於偽裝圓謊的假獵人

誰都不耐煩傾聽

只不過驚動了一下大地

山終於嚎啕起來

被吞噬的人不知道

倉皇逃難的人不知道

徬徨無依的人也不知道

紛紛的落石是山的眼淚

1999.10.01

Mountain in Tears

Mountain in tears, could you hear it

Nobody is listening

Nobody knows that mountain is crying

Modern people do not understand the mountain

They do not know that mountain might be thirsty and

    weeping

They do not know that mountain might be pain, itch

    or ache

They rather imagine that

        stream is mountain at whispering

        waterfall is mountain at singing

But could you hear that mountain is crying

The pirate woodcutters arbitrarily destroy the mountain

pretending skillfully as good liars of phony hunters

However, nobody would be patient enough to listen

When the earth is suffered from a bit of quake

the mountain falls to wailing

The people buried alive do not know

the people fleeing in panic do not know

the people wandering in helpless do not know

that continuous falling rocks are the tears of mountain

1999

問　天

房子倒了之後

還有帳篷

帳篷倒了之後呢

大人傷亡了之後

還有小孩

小孩傷亡了之後呢

政府挨罵了之後

還有在野黨

在野黨挨罵了之後呢

地震災害了之後

還有颱風

颱風災害了之後呢

1999.10.09

Asking the Heaven

After the houses collapse

there are tents

what will be after the tents

After the adults injure and die

there are children

what will be after the children

After the government is blamed

there is opposition party

what will be after the opposition party

After the earthquake causes disaster

there is typhoon

what will be after the typhoon

1999

我習慣在廢紙上寫詩

我習慣在廢紙上寫詩

詩的優美和崇高表現

在文本　不在載體

這是簡單不過的道理

有人關心台灣的環境污染

用雪銅紙印出垃圾滿地的場景

在精美的媒體上呈現滿目瘡痍

不惜浪費生態資源

合理化攻擊生態破壞者

台灣幾時已落入自我消解顛覆的困境

詩要在醜中見美　死裡求生

於污穢地基上植被難見的優雅

你要知道　有人用文字寫詩

有人用生產和勞動唱出詩的內涵

有人用生命填補史詩的空白

詩也是意義的實踐　不止是美

任何形式的浪費都是非詩的行為

我並不刻意選用廢紙寫詩

只是要你知道　滿足於克己的習慣

奉行少增加台灣負擔的傾心

2000.01.30

I used to write Poem on Waste Paper

I used to write poem on waste paper

The beauty and sublime of a poem

exist in the text itself rather than in the media

This is a truth quite simple enough

Someone are concerned about environmental pollution

They print on brilliant nice paper with garbage scenes

stained with dirt all over the elegant media

not stingy in wasting natural resources

justifying their attack on ecological destroyers

As Taiwan falls into self-dissolution and self-
subversion dilemma

a poem aims to find beauty in ugliness, and life in
death
to plant rare gracefulness in the nasty ground
One should know some write poems in literal sense
some sing the substance of poem with labor and
production
and some fill up the blank of epics with their lives

A poem is also the presentation of meanings not only
beauty
Any form of waste is a non-poetical act
I do not intend to write poem on waste paper

but just want to carry out the habit of self-restraint

and willing to less increasing the burden on the Earth

2000

海　韻

電話交談中

忽聞海浪衝擊聲

無端澎湃來

2000.03.12

Sea Rhythm

Chatting over phone

I hear sudden swashing waves

surging over me

2000

五月的形影

在庭院裡

看到一朵玫瑰杜鵑苞蕾

在風中掙扎綻放時

想起了五月

在樓頂上

眺望一艘遊歷四海的輪船

在水平線上迎風駛過時

想起了五月

情人節到來時

心中理想的形影

像候鳥一般隨風遠飛

準備上街參加反核遊行吧

心想一大把年紀了

愛情和形骸都不能久留

那就遺愛人間吧

摘下初開的玫瑰杜鵑

在樓頂上

久久望著漸漸駛離視線的輪船

極目看不到五月的形影

呈獻

2001.02.12

Figure in May

In the courtyard

my eyes gleam an rosy azalea in bud

laboring to burst out in the wind

redolent of May

Upstairs

I look at distance a steamer navigating around the
    oceans

sailing across the horizon against the wind

redolent of May

On Saint Valentine's Day

my idolized figure is just like

a migratory bird soaring with the wind

I prepare to join the anti-nuclear demonstration on street

but think that in my quite old age

neither love nor body can persist long

it had better bequeath them to the world

Plucking the blooming rosy azalea

upstairs

I gaze at the steamer sailing away from my sight

until the figure in May is lost to my view

to dedicate

2001

秋 池

風吹

魚紛紛

飛入池塘裡

色彩斑斕的魚

浮在水面上

望著天空

終究

要丟棄

人間的形體吧

剩下一幅

魚骨造型般

鱗峋的葉脈

像歷史

透明

沉在池底

2003.10.27

The Pond in Autumn

When it blows

the fish flies pell-mell

into the pond

The colorful fish

floats on the water

staring at the sky

After all

should it discard

the form in the world

that leaves

the lean veins of leaves

in a pattern of fish bone

like history

settled transparently

on the bottom of pond

2003

克里希納

有人說祢是幽暗國度

我來到祢的懷裡

反而豁然開朗

知道世上竟有

那麼多人在生活水平以下

像蛆蟲在掙扎

那麼多人栖栖皇皇

比螞蟻忙碌和辛勞

那麼多灰塵蒙住天空

克里希納啊　祢的眼睛是否被蒙住

我常看見祢高高在上

注意崇拜祢的人來來往往

祢有沒有看透他的內心

有時激動　有時不安

有時需要撫慰　有時需要愛

幾千年的歷史從傳統進入現實

還有多少年可以把現實帶入夢境

祢在廟堂上我崇拜祢

我更嚮往祢在身邊讓我愛祢

我會像恆河穿透祢的心臟

說說人民的喜怒哀樂

和祢共享隨時感受的情意

印度或許有過幽暗的時代

光在誰的手裡呢

克里希納啊　祢張開著眼睛

天空有時灰濛　有時藍得晶瑩

就像我對袮一樣純淨

崇拜袮　我不用信徒的姿勢

我只是常常凝視袮

期待袮始終在我身邊

印度假使是幽暗

因為人的心還沒有打開

歷史的腳步很慢

我祈求成為袮的唯一

儘管袮還要照顧他人

我看到許多哀愁的眼睛

在車潮人潮中滿懷希望和憂傷

那些應該在快樂歲月的孩童

無助地張望人來人往

累積生活的重壓成長

他們需要祢　克里希納啊

更甚於我的心靈

我只要遠遠看祢一眼就心安

在祢身邊是緣份嗎

我終必回到軌道上應有的位置

印度會在我夢中時時出現

或許再過幾十年幾百年

我看到祢的時候

祢展露美麗的珍珠笑容

開光在印度人民幽暗的心坎上

2003.12.08晨5:50
印度奧蘭卡巴旅邸

Krishna

Someone supposed you were an area of darkness

I come into your bosom

and suddenly find bright instead

I wonder that in the world

how can so many people live under such lowest
  standard

struggling for existence like the maggots

so many people anxiously go around

more busy and more industrious than the ants

and so many floating dusts obscure the sky

Oh, Krishna, are your eyes shielded

I frequently notice that you are at high position

looking about your worshippers wandering to and fro

Do you see through their respective heart

sometime exciting, sometime uneasy

sometime expecting for consolation, sometime thirsty

    for love

In the history of thousands of year from tradition to

    the present

how many realities still can be brought into dreamland

I worship you at high status in the temple

I am more longing for staying close by to love you

I will resembles the Ganges River passing through

    your heart

telling you about the pleasure, anger, sorrow and joy

    of the people

to share with you enjoying passion of feeling at all

> *times*

India probably has a period of darkness

but who holds the light in hand

Oh, Krishna, please open your wide eyes

The sky is sometime gray, sometime crystalline azure

just like me so pure toward you

expressing my worship without pretending any

> *gesture of a disciple*

I am simply gazing at you from time to time

and hopeful of you always beside me

Supposedly, India was in darkness

because the hearts of people have not been opened yet

The steps of history are very slow

I pray for becoming your sole favorite

although you ought to take care of others

I observe numerous eyesight of sadness

full of hopes and distresses, among the tides of
vehicles and crowds

Those children who should be in happy years

helplessly looks at the masses coming and going

and growing up under the accumulated burden of
livelihood

They need you, oh, Krishna

more than my mind

I would be calm down just cast a look at you afar

Is it an affinity bring me to your side

I certainly must return to my position-should-be on

　　the orbit

yet India will appear in my dream constantly

Perhaps after some tens or hundreds of year

when I meet you again

you will display a smile of beautiful pearl

enlightened in the heart of darkness from Indian

　　people

2003

成吉思汗的夢

你有一個夢　龐大到

戈壁容不下　草原容不下

整個千禧年也容不下

遊牧的金星引導你

向北走　向東走　向南走

最後向西走　一直走到

天邊　一直走到海角

沙漠連接到茫茫海洋

草原進入到莽莽山林

你的夢在於歐亞拼圖

遊牧民族不收藏土地

取諸世界　還諸世界

你的蒙古馬是一顆流星

你的馬上雄姿眾人仰望

所到之處歷史成為流言

你忽而現身忽而消失

須臾　成就你的須彌

第二千禧年以你為尊

你的肉體化成幻影

宇宙間自由自在無所不在

你生諸天地　還諸天地

留下畫像流落未登臨過

海角島嶼台灣的虛擬故宮

繼續一個鄉愁的夢

夢到蒙古草原　夢到戈壁

夢到蒙古繁衍的子孫後裔

2005.07.29

Chinggis Khaan's Dream

You had a dream too huge to be confined

to the big Gobi, to the great steppe

even to whole Second Millennium

The nomadic Mars led you marching

northwards, eastwards, southwards

and finally westwards, all through until

the heaven margin, the sea cape

The desert was extended to the boundless oceans

the steppe was prolonged into the indefinite forests

Your dream was to combine Europe and Asia

The nomadic tribe did not collect the lands

which were returned to the world where taken from

Your Mongolian horse was just like a meteor

Your gesture on the horse was admired from the crowd

Wherever you reached the history turned to be a legend

You disappeared as soon as just appeared

A moment piled up to construct your Sumeru

You were honored as the Man in Second Millennium

Your body was vaporized becoming a vision

filled up within the Universe, everywhere and

   nowhere

You backed to the cosmos where you were born

There is your portrait exiled to a virtual palace

in Island Taiwan where you had never been

proceeding a continuous dream of nostalgia

to great Mongolian steppes, to the big Gobi

and to the prosperous Mongolian descendants

2005

愛　字

　　櫻花國度送來訊息的愛字

　　櫻花季節寄到的愛字

　　胭紅的油彩書寫的愛字

　　白色岩石間擠出鮮血的愛字

　　溫柔的和紙中傳遞的愛字

　　巧思尋求回應的愛字

　　越洋展演藝術交流的愛字

　　相約在威尼斯雙年展中會面的愛字

　　靜靜沒有聲音的愛字

　　心谷中不時迴盪的愛字

　　陌生人不忮不求的愛字

　　為了宣揚人類愛的愛字

　　　　　　　　　　　　　　　2005.04.15

LOVE Letter

LOVE message from the country of cherry blossom

LOVE arrived in the season of cherry blossom

LOVE written with oil paint of pink color

LOVE in blood squeezed out of white rock

LOVE transmitted in an envelope of wa-shi paper*

LOVE looking for response in sophisticated design

LOVE exhibiting artistic communication over ocean

LOVE looking forward for meeting in Venice biennale

LOVE in silence without any sound

LOVE finding an echo in deep valley of heart

LOVE neither refusing nor pursuing for a stranger

LOVE for promoting human LOVE

2005

Note: A kind of characteristic Japanese paper

有鳥飛過

六歲的小孩

在車上一再叮嚀

前面有鳥飛過

小心不要撞到

等一下又說

有蝴蝶

小心蝴蝶

不要撞到

我說放心啦

看到螞蟻

我也會停車

讓螞蟻慢慢走過

還有細菌呢

他有些憂心地說

還有細菌呢

怎麼辦

2005.09.12

Birds Flying Over

The child of six-year old

reiterates in my car

be careful about

the birds flying over ahead

After a while he says again

there are butterflies

be careful about butterflies

do not hit on them

I reply do not worry

even I notice the ants

I will stop the car

let them pass by slowly

Then the bacteria

he whispers anxiously

then the bacteria

how to avoid them

2005

在格瑞納達

在我的故鄉

經常聽到

心靈的呼喚

來自尼加拉瓜

達里奧的祖國

絲絲入扣

從太平洋此岸

到達台灣東海岸

從世紀的此岸

到達時間流逝的彼岸

從現實世界的此岸

到夢裡尋尋覓覓的彼岸

循著心靈的呼喚

終於來到尼加拉瓜

我看到達里奧的同胞

在太陽豐收的土地上

有著褐色的笑容

在古城格瑞納達

從世紀遠遠的彼岸

流傳著美麗與哀愁

從世界各國匯流

詩的友誼和夢幻

2006.02.07
尼加拉瓜格瑞納達

In Granada

In my homeland

I frequently hear

the calling of mind

from Nicaragua

the fatherland of Dario

depth in my heart

from this side of Pacific coast

to the eastern coast of Taiwan

from this side of the century

to the other coast of time elapsed

from this shore of real world

to that sought in the dream

I follow the calling of mind

arriving at Nicaragua eventually

I see the people of Dario

exhibiting their brown smiles

on the fertile sunny land

In Granada, the old city

beauty and sorrow streaming

far, far from other coast of the century

friendship and dream through poetry

converging from the countries all over the world

2006

雪落大草原

蒙古包外

雪靜靜落著

天地柔情對話有滿月見證

蒙古包內

劈拍響的燒柴正熾

旅人的心跳聲應和著

旅人們圍著爐火的談興

追憶年輕時的豪邁

對照進入老境的心情

蒙古包內

漸起的鼾聲流水般

時而悠揚時而徐緩

蒙古包外

大草原的雪

跳起了迴旋土風舞

2006.09.12

Snow is Falling on the Steppe

Outside the ger[1]

Snow is falling on the steppe

The dialogue between heaven and earth is verified by

the full moon

Inside the ger

the burning of firewood claps vigorously

the beating of traveler heart responds

The travelers around the fireplace chat

vivid in the memory of young splendor

comparing now the feeling of aged mood

Inside the ger

the rising snores flow like a stream

sometime violent and sometime slow

Outside the ger

snow on the steppe

is dancing the folk dance in rondo

2006

---

1. yurt in Mongolian

Index of Titles

E

Y

詩題索引

李魁賢簡歷

　　1937年6月19日生於台北市。1945年於二次世界大戰末期，回到祖籍台北縣淡水鎮。現居台北市。1958年畢業於台北工業專科學校（現台北科技大學），主修化學工程；1964年結業於教育部歐洲語文中心，主修德文。1985年獲美國*Marquis Giuseppe Sciencluna*國際大學基金會頒授榮譽化工哲學博士學位。

　　曾任台肥公司南港廠值班主管、製法工程師以及工場副主任（1960-1968），後來從事專利代辦業務（1968-1974）。創立名流企業有限公司（1975-2003）、名流出版社（1986-1989）和名流專利事務所（1987-1988）。擔任發明雜誌編輯（1969-1971）、發明天地雜誌社長（1974-1975）、台灣省發明人協會常務理事（1977-1986）、發明

企業雜誌發行人（1979-1987），歷任台灣筆會
副會長（1987-1989）、理事（1989-1994）、會
長（1995-1996），國立台灣師範大學人文講席
（2001），淡水文化基金會董事（2001-2005），
台灣北社社務委員（2001-2002）、副社長
（2002-2003），國家文化藝術基金會董事
（2001-2004）、董事長（2005-2007），國立中正大
學台灣文學研究所兼任教授（2006-2007）。

　　1953年開始發表詩作，獲1967年優秀詩人獎、
1975年吳濁流新詩獎、1975年中山技術發明獎、1976
年英國國際詩人學會傑出詩人獎、1978年中興文藝獎
章詩歌獎、1982年義大利藝術大學文學傑出獎、1983
年比利時布魯塞爾市長金質獎章、1984年笠詩評論
獎、1986年美國愛因斯坦國際學術基金會和平銅牌
獎、1986年巫永福評論獎、1993年韓國亞洲詩人貢
獻獎、1994年笠詩創作獎、1994年榮後台灣詩獎、
1998年印度國際詩人年度最佳詩人獎、2000年印度
國際詩人學會千禧年詩人獎、2001年賴和文學獎、

2001年行政院文化獎、2002年印度麥氏學會（Michael Madhusudan Academy）詩人獎、2002年台灣新文學貢獻獎、2004年吳三連獎新詩獎、2004年印度國際詩人亞洲之星獎、2005年蒙古文化基金會文化名人獎牌和詩人獎章、2006年蒙古建國八百週年成吉思汗金牌、成吉思汗大學金質獎章和蒙古作家聯盟推廣蒙古文學貢獻獎。2001年、2003年、2006年三度被印度國際詩人團體提名為諾貝爾文學獎候選人。

詩被翻譯在日本、韓國、加拿大、紐西蘭、荷蘭、南斯拉夫、羅馬尼亞、印度、希臘、美國、西班牙、蒙古等國發表。參加過韓國、日本、印度、蒙古、薩爾瓦多、尼加拉瓜、美國等國之國際詩歌節。

出版有《李魁賢詩集》六冊（2001年）、《李魁賢文集》十冊（2002年）、《李魁賢譯詩集》八冊（2003年）、《歐洲經典詩選》（2001-2005年）等。

About the Auther

Lee Kuei-shien (b. 1937-) graduated from Taipei Institute of Technology. He began to write poems in 1953, became a member of the International Academy of Poets in England in 1976, and joined to establish the Taiwan P.E.N. in 1987 and was elected as Vice-President and then President.

His poems have been translated and published in Japan, Korea, Canada, New Zealand, Netherlands, Yugoslavia, Romania, India, Greece, Spain, Mongolia and Russia.

Published works include "Collected Poems" in six volumes (2001), "Collected Essays" in ten volumes (2002), "Translated Poems" in eight volumes (2003),"Anthology of European Poetry" in 25 volumes (2001~2005)and others, including "Golden Treasury of Modern Indian Poetry" (2005) in which the poems by former President A.P.J. Abdul Kalam are included.

Awarded with Merit of Asian Poet, Korea (1994), Rong-hou Taiwanese Poet Prize (1997), World Poet of the Year 1997, Poets International, India (1998), Poet of the Millennium Award , International poets Academy , India (2000), Lai Ho Literature Prize and Premier Culture Prize , both in Taiwan (2001) and nominated as a candidate for the Nobel Prize in Literature, by International Poets Academy, India. He also received the Michael Madhusudan Poet Award from the Michael Madhusudan Academy (2002), Wu San-lien Prize in Literature (2004)and Poet Medal from Mongolian Cultural Foundation (2005).

He has attended the international poetry festivals held in Korea, Japan, India, Mongolia, U.S.A. , E1 Salvador and Nicaragua .

國家圖書館出版品預行編目

黃昏時刻 / 李魁賢作. -- 一版. -- 臺北市：
秀威資訊科技, 2010.01
　　面；　公分. -- （語言文學類；PG0305）

BOD版
含索引
ISBN 978-986-221-273-8 （平裝）

851.486　　　　　　　　　　　　98013122

語言文學類　PG0305

黃昏時刻

作　　　者 / 李魁賢
發　行　人 / 宋政坤
執 行 編 輯 / 藍志成
圖 文 排 版 / 鄭維心
封 面 設 計 / 陳佩蓉
數 位 轉 譯 / 徐真玉　沈裕閔
圖 書 銷 售 / 林怡君
法 律 顧 問 / 毛國樑　律師
出 版 印 製 / 秀威資訊科技股份有限公司
　　　　　　台北市內湖區瑞光路583巷25號1樓
　　　　　　電話：02-2657-9211　傳真：02-2657-9106
　　　　　　E-mail：service@showwe.com.tw
經　　銷　商 / 紅螞蟻圖書有限公司
　　　　　　台北市內湖區舊宗路二段121巷28、32號4樓
　　　　　　電話：02-2795-3656　傳真：02-2795-4100
　　　　　　http://www.e-redant.com

2010 年 1 月　BOD 一版
定價： 390 元

讀 者 回 函 卡

感謝您購買本書,為提升服務品質,煩請填寫以下問卷,收到您的寶貴意見後,我們會仔細收藏記錄並回贈紀念品,謝謝!

1.您購買的書名:＿＿＿＿＿＿＿＿＿＿＿＿＿＿＿＿＿

2.您從何得知本書的消息?

　　□網路書店　　□部落格　　□資料庫搜尋　　□書訊　　□電子報　　□書店

　　□平面媒體　　□ 朋友推薦　　□網站推薦 □其他＿＿＿＿＿＿

3.您對本書的評價:(請填代號　1.非常滿意 2.滿意 3.尚可 4.再改進)

　　封面設計＿＿　 版面編排＿＿＿　 內容＿＿　 文/譯筆＿＿＿　 價格＿＿

4.讀完書後您覺得:

　　□很有收獲　　□有收獲　　□收獲不多　　□沒收獲

5.您會推薦本書給朋友嗎?

　　□會　□不會,為什麼?＿＿＿＿＿＿＿＿＿＿＿＿＿＿＿＿

6.其他寶貴的意見:＿＿＿＿＿＿＿＿＿＿＿＿＿＿＿＿＿

＿＿＿＿＿＿＿＿＿＿＿＿＿＿＿＿＿＿＿＿＿＿＿＿＿＿＿

＿＿＿＿＿＿＿＿＿＿＿＿＿＿＿＿＿＿＿＿＿＿＿＿＿＿＿

＿＿＿＿＿＿＿＿＿＿＿＿＿＿＿＿＿＿＿＿＿＿＿＿＿＿＿

讀者基本資料

姓名:＿＿＿＿＿＿＿＿＿＿＿　 年齡:＿＿＿＿　 性別:□女 □男

聯絡電話:＿＿＿＿＿＿＿＿＿　 E-mail:＿＿＿＿＿＿＿＿＿＿

地址:＿＿＿＿＿＿＿＿＿＿＿＿＿＿＿＿＿＿＿＿＿＿＿＿

學歷:□高中(含)以下　　□高中　　□專科學校　　□大學

　　　□研究所(含)以上 □其他＿＿＿＿＿＿＿

職業:□製造業 □金融業 □資訊業 □軍警 □傳播業 □自由業

　　　□服務業 □公務員 □教職　 □學生 □其他＿＿＿＿＿

To：114

台北市內湖區瑞光路 583 巷 25 號 1 樓

秀威資訊科技股份有限公司　　　收

寄件人姓名：

寄件人地址：□□□

秀威與 BOD

BOD（Books On Demand）是數位出版的大趨勢，秀威資訊率先運用 POD 數位印刷設備來生產書籍，並提供作者全程數位出版服務，致使書籍產銷零庫存，知識傳承不絕版，目前已開闢以下書系：

一、BOD 學術著作—專業論述的閱讀延伸
二、BOD 個人著作—分享生命的心路歷程
三、BOD 旅遊著作—個人深度旅遊文學創作
四、BOD 大陸學者—大陸專業學者學術出版
五、POD 獨家經銷—數位產製的代發行書籍

BOD 秀威網路書店：www.showwe.com.tw
政府出版品網路書店：www.govbooks.com.tw

永不絕版的故事・自己寫・永不休止的音符・自己唱